I REMEMBER

Treveon Roseberry

I Remember. Copyright 2023 by Author. All rights reserved. No part of this publication may be reproduced, distributed, or transmitted in any form or by any means, including photocopying, recording, or other electronic or mechanical methods, without the prior written permission of the publisher, except in the case of brief quotations embodied in critical reviews and certain other noncommercial uses permitted by copyright law.

For permission requests, write to the publisher, addressed "Attention: Permissions Coordinator," 205 N. Michigan Avenue, Suite #810, Chicago, IL 60601. 13th & Joan books may be purchased for educational, business or sales promotional use. For information, please email the Sales Department at sales@13thandjoan.com.

Printed in the U. S. A.

First Printing, July 2023.

Library of Congress Cataloging-in-Publication Data has been applied for.

ISBN: 978-1-7322479-1-8

Dedicated to Winnie Mae Campbell —

My nanny, a true matriarch
whose shoulders I stand tall on today.

Preface

I Remember… is a story about a woman who helped shape the lives of so many people around her, including mine. Winnie Mae Campbell was born on June 26, 1932, in Colorado City, TX; the 9th born of 15, to Cleveland and Minnie Parks. At just 15, Winnie married the love of her life and stayed that way, married and in love with life, for the next 66 years before losing her fight with Alzheimer's disease.

I wanted to tell her story in a way that showed the world that one person can truly have an impact on the world and in the lives of those in it. I also wanted my nieces, Harmony and Haileigh, to know the woman I got to experience – their great-great grandmother. There are so many lessons that I learned growing up with my nanny, but the real lesson is that people remember how you made them feel, and not always the moments you made them feel them in.

This story is loosely based on an experience that I shared with my great grandmother, Winnie Mae Campbell, "Nanny" to some.

Today was a day like no other before it. There were birds chirping, frogs croaking, and the sun had just peeked over the horizon, rising slowly.

A visit to see my great grandmother was on the agenda and picking peas in the fields was the memory to be made.

But first, my nanny had to paint her turtles.

She fed her new friends and gave them new names. Each one got a letter on its shell and a place to call home.

It's how she recognized the old ones from the newbies.

They'd leave each day but come back the next for more. They'd always remember the right house to pick and show up daily, belly empty, ready to get full as a tick.

After the meeting with her hard-shelled friends, we hopped in the car and drove for a bit. Just up the road, for only a few minutes.

The west Texas air was crisp and clean, and tumbleweeds rolled through crosswalks while the stop lights turned red, bringing us to a stop.

We made a right turn where we usually make a left, and I was confused. "What is this?" I asked Nanny.

She was disoriented and looked a little lost. "It's okay baby, sometimes I just forget." We paused to regroup, turned back the right way, made it to the fields, and started our day.

Nanny showed me which peas to pick, teaching me lessons about life as we went, sharing her knowledge and telling stories of inequity during her life.

She shared vivid memories and did it with such poise.

When we finished up, we made our way home the same way we came, except for this time without error.

We turned down Dormard, the street where she lived. It wasn't the house on the corner, but the second one with red brick.

The front yard was small with a great big tree that bore fruit. But not the kind you might think. These were pecans, best in a pie or alone, but fun to crack open and eat right out of the shell.

The front door flew open, and I grinned really big. I got to see my great grandfather, my aunt, and some other folks as I made my way to the den. Nanny's house was the place to be and the whole family knew it.

The peas in these pods needed to be shelled. My nanny ran her fingers through the green glossy skin that housed the peas we wanted, each one ringing out as it landed in the bucket.

The buckets became full, and the conversations began to die down.

It was time to cook!

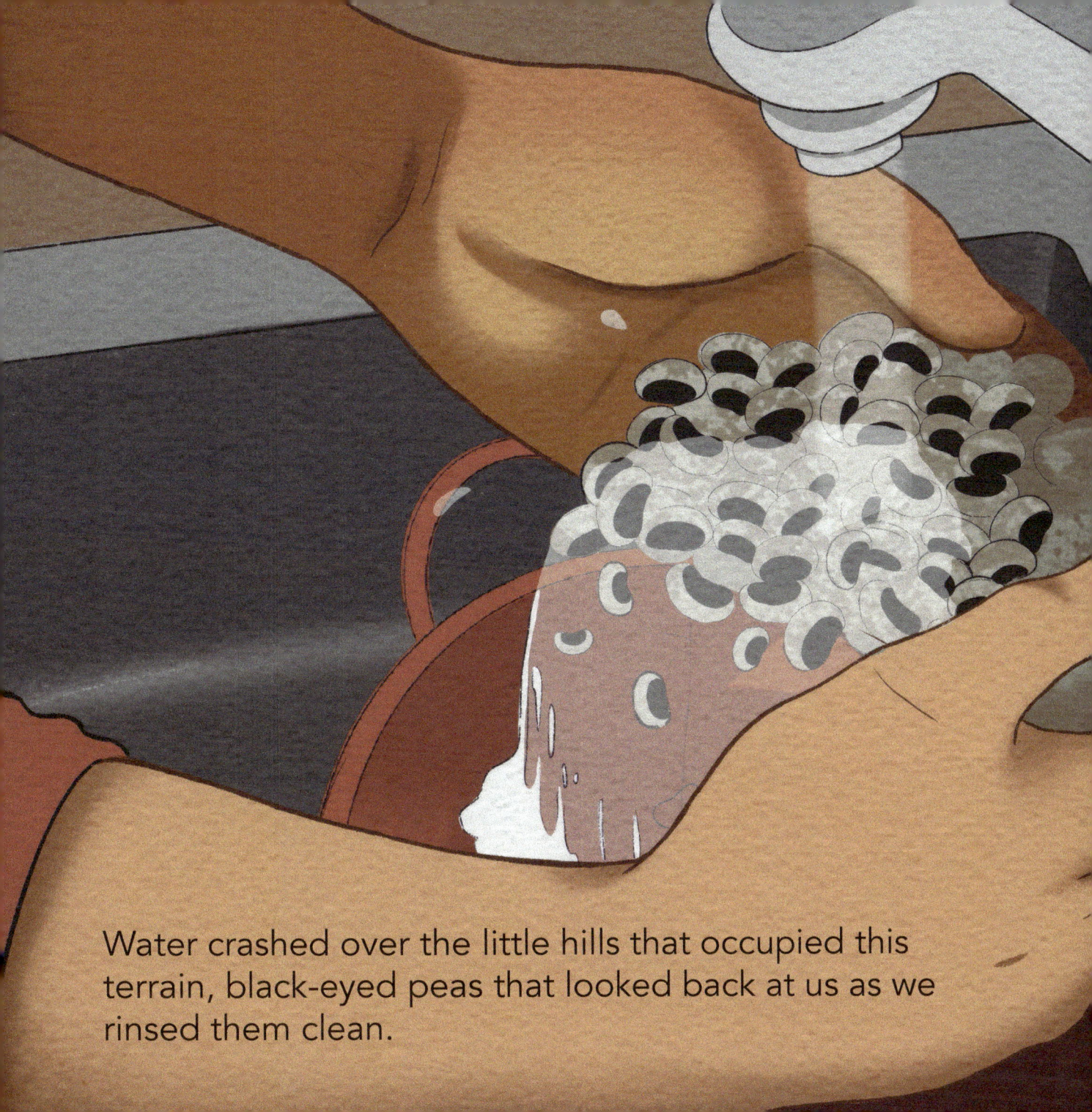

Water crashed over the little hills that occupied this terrain, black-eyed peas that looked back at us as we rinsed them clean.

I smiled from the joy I felt, but also noticed the dazed look that was on my great-grandmother's face.

She was physically there, but her mind had wandered.

Maybe it was back in the fields that we had just left, or in a time before today. Wherever it was, it wasn't present. It wasn't in *this* moment.

Nanny finally came back from where she had gone to continue her lesson, and really show me how black-eyed peas were done.

She poured them from one pot to another, added water and her own special seasoning that was hidden at the back of the shelf.

The packaging on the seasoning was simple — "special seasoning." It was super nondescript.

She added some of this special stuff, tasted the broth, and added a bit more.

Some hours passed as we left the food to broil and bake as we rested from the day's work.

We waited, laughed and giggled, told our favorite stories, and waited some more.

Then finally...it was time to eat!

This wasn't just food that would nourish our bodies, but it was food that would attach itself to our souls and hearts. Making us feel loved and warm inside.

It wasn't the recipe that made the food special, it was my nanny who brought special to the recipe.

We ate and turned in for the night.

We'd leave tomorrow and head back home.

We woke up early, before 4am.

My grandmother, my nanny's daughter, would warm up the car and we'd start our 7 or 8 hour journey back to Houston, where we lived.

Many years passed before we went back to visit. I grew older and so did my nanny. By this time, I was a teenager.

Grandma and I packed up the car the same way we did before, made lunches for the drive, and were on our way. We listened to old cassette tapes and sang all the way there.

7 to 8 hours later we had almost made it to our final stop. We turned down Dormard, the street where my nanny lived. It wasn't the house on the corner, but the second one, with red brick.

I hopped out of the car and ran to the door. I didn't need to knock because it was always open.

I entered with a grin and made the hike down the hall, speaking to everyone who was there on my way to the den.

There she was. Sitting in her chair that rocked, beautifully made up like the true matriarch she was.

I hugged her neck tight to make up for the time that I had been away and told her how happy I was to see her.

I could see that her eyes were different this time. They lacked the passion that had once occupied them. She asked who I was and where I had gotten all of my energy. I said, "It's me, Terrell."

"Terrell?" she asked.

"I'm your great-grandson," I replied.

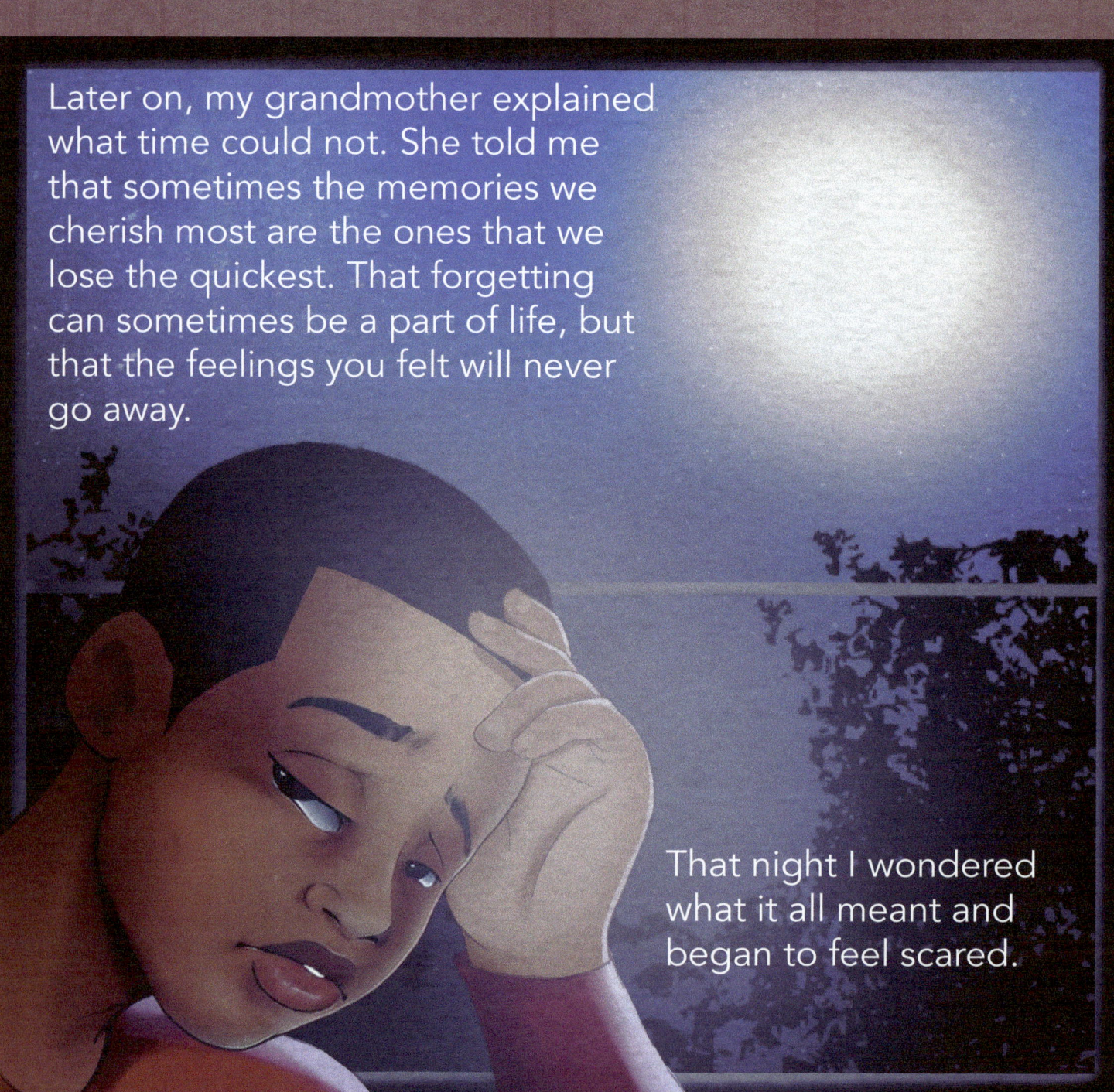

Later on, my grandmother explained what time could not. She told me that sometimes the memories we cherish most are the ones that we lose the quickest. That forgetting can sometimes be a part of life, but that the feelings you felt will never go away.

That night I wondered what it all meant and began to feel scared.

We woke up the next morning to the smell of coffee and pancakes. We ate breakfast on the patio and like clockwork, the turtles began to appear.

It reminded me that even though Nanny didn't remember, they did.

Nanny called my name and asked me a series of questions; "Do you have any kids yet? You married?" I responded, "No, none of those things." And even though the questions came a little bit out of the blue, I was most excited that, even for just a moment, she remembered me.

I smiled and hugged her tighter than I had before. My grandmother finally pulled me aside and told me that Nanny had Alzheimer's.

She explained that it was a disease that affected a person's ability to recall and remember.

At first I didn't understand, and it was hard to hear, but I was just happy to be next to a woman who had created so much life, so many memories, and who had helped to shape my future without any knowledge of how it would turn out.

We left the next day, and this time I hugged her even tighter than before. She didn't remember who I was, but I wanted to make sure that she *felt* every bit of who I am.

Another year would pass, and I grew older.

We packed up the car the same way we did before, made lunches for the drive, and were on our way.

And for the final time, we turned down Dormard, the street where my nanny had lived. It wasn't the house on the corner, but the second one with red brick.

This time though, she wasn't there.

And while she didn't live forever, she planted something in me and my family that would.

She reminded us that the harvest doesn't come immediately after you plant the seeds. It comes when it's time to harvest.

And while my nanny had no more seasons to endure, she made sure that we were prepared for ours by teaching us and building our capacity to receive a true harvest.

We may have only picked peas, but the true fruit was new life.

Treveon Roseberry is a Houston native and University of Houston alumnus who has always had a passion for storytelling. From an early age, he was drawn to the power of words and their ability to inspire, motivate and comfort.

In this debut book, Treveon tells a story of tribute to the women who have made a difference in his life and the lives of others. This is a celebration of their strength, resilience, and determination, and serves as a reminder of the power of the human spirit and mind.

Printed in the USA
CPSIA information can be obtained
at www.ICGtesting.com
LVHW072158031123
762894LV00014B/830